Tweenies™

Caterpillar Surprise

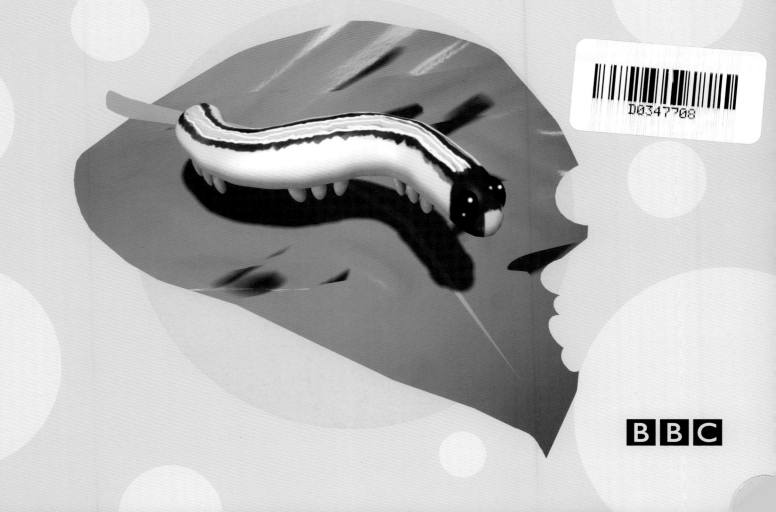

BBC

One day, Max went to visit a meadow. When he got back, the Tweenies wanted to know all about the things he had seen there.

"What did you see in the meadow, Max?" asked Fizz. "Well, I saw some lovely wild flowers, some trees and lots of birds," Max replied.

"Did you bring anything back with you?" asked Milo.

"Do you know, I think I brought back some ants in my pants," replied Max, wriggling a bit.

That made Bella, Milo, Fizz and Jake giggle.

"What else did you see in the meadow, Max?" asked Jake.
"Did you see any tigers or elephants?" asked Milo.

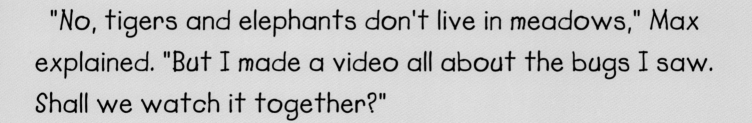

"No, tigers and elephants don't live in meadows," Max explained. "But I made a video all about the bugs I saw. Shall we watch it together?"

Fizz pressed the button on the Tweenie clock.

"Telly time!" she shouted.

Then they all settled down in front of the telly.

"Look!" said Milo. "There's a spider."

"That's right," Max replied. "I saw lots of spiders."

"What's that creepy-crawly?" asked Jake, looking closely at the screen.

"That's a caterpillar, Jake. What else can you see?" asked Max.

"I can see a ladybird," said Fizz.

"Did you see any butterflies?" Bella asked. "I like butterflies."

"No, I didn't see any butterflies in the meadow today, Bella," replied Max.

"Oh," said Bella sadly.

"I know. Why don't we look for bugs in the garden?" suggested Max.

"Good idea, Max," agreed the Tweenies.

The Tweenies and Max went into the garden and looked closely to see if they could spy anything crawling under the bushes or munching on the leaves.

"I can't see anything," said Milo.

"Neither can I," said Fizz. "It's just trees and twigs and grass."

"Oh, I can see something on that leaf," said Jake. "It looks like a jelly bean."

"That's not a jelly bean," said Bella. "It's a cocoon. There's a caterpillar inside it, and when it grows up it turns into something wonderful. We know a song about it... don't we, Max!"

Caterpillar walking,
Up and down the trees.

Caterpillar munching,
On the tasty leaves.

Caterpillar hiding,
Nowhere to be found.

Caterpillar sleeping,
Safe and sound.

"What happens next, Max?" asked
Milo. "Does the caterpillar wake up?"
"Well, Milo, the caterpillar does
wake up, in a way," replied Max.
"Let me explain."

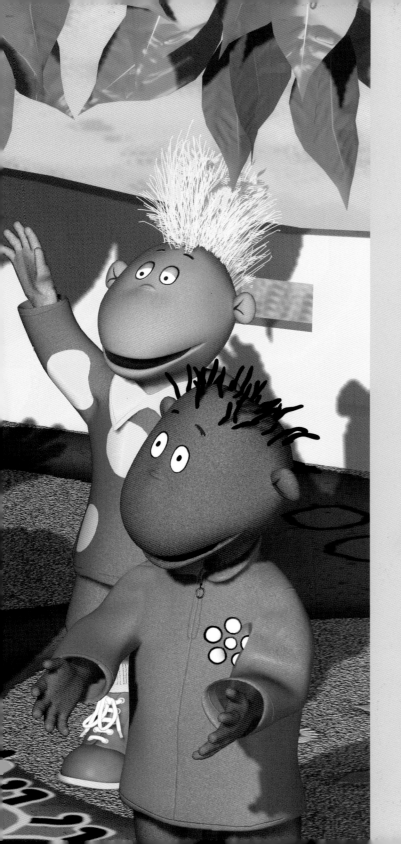

"First, a baby caterpillar grows from an egg. When the caterpillar gets bigger, it changes into something else."

"I know," said Bella. "The caterpillar changes into a..."

"Shhh, Bella!" said Max suddenly. "Let's keep the next bit a secret so that the change is a surprise."

"Can we take the cocoon inside?" asked Fizz.

"I think we should leave it here where it belongs. We can come and see it every day," replied Max.

Max went off to read the paper and the Tweenies went off to find different things to do.

Jake painted a picture of a caterpillar and Fizz drew a picture of a ladybird. Bella read a book about butterflies.

But Milo started to
wonder just what was
going to happen when the
caterpillar woke up.

Milo went outside
and peered under the leaf
at the cocoon. He thought
he saw it move, but nothing
much else happened.

"When are we going
to get our surprise?"
he wondered.

Then Fizz went outside
to see if anything had
happened to the cocoon,
but it still looked exactly
the same.

"Where's the surprise?"
thought Fizz.

Later, Jake went outside to see if the caterpillar had woken up yet. But all he could see was the little cocoon dangling from the leaf.

"It's not much of a surprise," thought Jake.

Only Bella stayed away from the garden. She knew that you had to be patient if you wanted to enjoy this surprise. She carried on reading her book. It had some lovely pictures in it.

The next day, the day after and the day after that, there was still no sign of the caterpillar waking up. Then, early one morning, Max called Bella into the garden.

The cocoon had broken open! The outsides of the caterpillar's silky coat fell to the ground. Something small and crumpled held on tightly to the leaf.

"Oh, Max, isn't it lovely?" smiled Bella, as the small crumpled thing opened up slowly and stretched its wings.

The other Tweenies came
out to see what it was.

"Oh, it's a flutterby!" cried Jake.

"You mean a butterfly," said Fizz.

"Wow, what a great surprise!" cried Milo.

"Now we can sing the rest of the song,
Max," said Bella.

Caterpillar waking,
Looks up at the sky.

Opens out her wings,
And becomes a butterfly!

"Bye-bye butterfly!" The Tweenies waved goodbye to the beautiful butterfly as it fluttered away, over their heads and up, up, up into the sky.

THE END